AT THE STROKE OF ONE, THE ENORMOUS CUCKOO CLOCK BEGINS TO CHIME.

Slowly, the huge door above the dial begins to creak open. Inside, all is black, except for a pair of shining green eyes peering out.

Suddenly a huge robot bird shoots out of the small doorway. It hovers over the room for a moment, as if searching out its prey. Then the bird swoops down, grabs Lois with its sharp metal claws, and streaks out the window!

Great Krypton! Clark thinks. *I've got to save Lois! But the clock is still ticking—it might be a bomb!!"*

If Clark switches to Superman and goes after Lois, continue on page 55.

If Clark examines the clock to see if it is a bomb, turn to page 57.

REMEMBER—WHAT SUPERMAN DOES IS UP TO YOU!

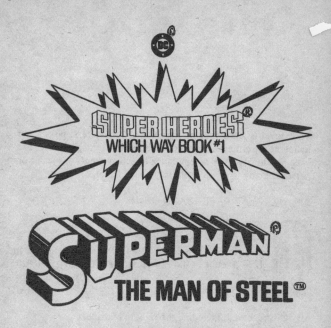

SUPER HEROES®
WHICH WAY BOOK #1

SUPERMAN®
THE MAN OF STEEL™

by Andrew Helfer
illustrated by José Delbo

AN ARCHWAY PAPERBACK
Published by POCKET BOOKS • NEW YORK

AN ARCHWAY PAPERBACK *Original*

An Archway Paperback published by
POCKET BOOKS, a division of Simon & Schuster, Inc.
1230 Avenue of the Americas, New York, N.Y. 10020

ISBN: 0-671-47463-4

First Archway Paperback printing June, 1983

10 9 8 7 6 5 4 3 2 1

Printed in the U.S.A.

IL   3+

To Colleen,
Richard,
Lewis,
and David
—my family and friends

Attention!

Super Heroes Which Way Books must be read in a special way. *Do not read the pages in order.* If you do, the story will make no sense at all. Instead, follow the directions at the bottom of each page until you come to an ending. Only then should you return to the beginning and start over again, making different choices this time.

In this book, *you* make the decisions for Superman. Some of your choices might lead to victory for the Man of Steel, others to defeat or doom. Of course, Superman himself would *always* make the correct choices to defeat the villains and save the day—but here, *you* control the Man of Steel. His fate is in *your* hands. Good luck!

It's a beautiful summer morning as Superman, the Man of Steel, soars high over the busy streets of Metropolis. Superman is on patrol, but it has been a quiet, uneventful day.

People on the streets below see Superman flying overhead. They wave happily, knowing that they are safe from danger—for they are protected by Earth's Mightiest Mortal!

Turn to page 2.

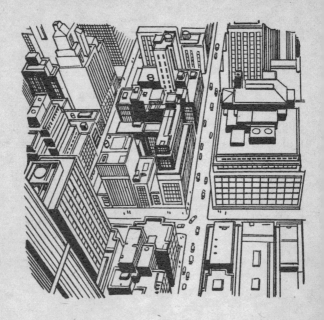

Well, it doesn't seem as if Metropolis is in any trouble today, Superman thinks. *There's not a thing to worry about here! Maybe I'll patrol some other cities—or perhaps I'll check in at the* Daily Planet.

If Superman decides to change into Clark Kent and stop by the Daily Planet, *continue on page 3.*

If Superman decides to fly toward another city, turn to page 4.

Superman flies down into an empty alleyway. There he changes into Clark Kent, mild-mannered reporter.

Within moments, Clark stands at the entrance to the *Daily Planet* newsroom. In front of him, busy reporters, editors, copy boys, and secretaries dash across the noisy, crowded office.

"Clark!" a woman shouts as she runs toward the reporter. "Perry White wants to see you in his office—pronto!"

"I wouldn't want to keep the boss waiting," Clark answers. "I'm on my way."

Turn to page 7.

As Superman flies across the country, he suddenly hears the sound of people screaming in terror.

The Man of Steel trains his telescopic vision on the source of the sounds. Then he sees it. There, in the center of a small town, a nine-foot yellow monster smashes through the streets, howling furiously as it crashes into building after building.

Superman must answer the call for help.

(continued on page 5)

The monster's rampage of destruction continues as, seconds later, Superman arrives. The nine-foot creature bellows horribly, almost painfully, as it swings its powerful arms.

Wasting no time, Superman swoops down upon the monster, grabs it by the arm, and begins to spin it in the air. Faster and faster the Man of Steel whirls about, and when he finally lets go, the creature flies off into space.

If Superman pursues the monster to destroy it, turn to page 6.

If Superman follows it to find out the monster's reason for wanting to destroy the town, turn to page 21.

In space, Superman catches up with the monster. The Man of Steel swings his fist with all his strength. As he lands a super-punch on the monster, a tremendous explosion rocks the sky, throwing Superman backward.

Dazed, Superman looks up and sees thousands of pieces of the shattered monster streaking down toward the planet. Using his telescopic vision, he sees that each piece is rapidly growing into a *new* creature! He knows that, within minutes, thousands of full-sized monsters will land on Earth. There are too many for even Superman to stop. The Earth is doomed.

The End

Clark walks briskly to Perry's office, but is stopped by Lois Lane, the *Planet*'s top reporter. The beautiful brown-eyed journalist looks excited.

"Clark!" she says breathlessly. "You simply *must* come over to my office! One of my fans has just sent me the *most* wonderful gift—it's got to be seen to be believed!"

"Well, Lois," Clark says, "I'd love to, but you see, Perry wants to see me—"

"Oh, Clark," Lois insists, "it'll only take a minute!"

If Clark takes a look at Lois' gift, turn to page 12.

If Clark goes directly to Perry's office, turn to page 8.

"Clark, I want you to see this," Editor-in-Chief Perry White says as Clark Kent steps into his office. On the television screen, master criminal Lex Luthor is about to speak.

"Greetings, Superman," Luthor says. "For months I have been working on my latest invention—an Ion Beam Death Ray capable of destroying the entire city of Metropolis in seconds. And destroy it I shall, Superman—unless *you* agree to come to the place where we first met. Farewell, Man of Steel—I await your arrival."

"Clark," Perry says as Luthor's image fades from the screen, "Luthor met Superman in Smallville. I want you to cover the story from there."

Perhaps Luthor is planning a trap for Superman, Clark thinks as he leaves Perry's office. *Maybe Clark Kent should find out what Luthor is up to.*

If Superman confronts Luthor in Smallville, continue on page 9.

If he investigates Luthor's plan first as Clark Kent, turn to page 20.

If you want to learn more about Luthor, check the Fortress file on page 117.

Soon the Man of Steel is flying over the city of Smallville.

He is on his way to the small laboratory on the outskirts of town that Lex Luthor used as a teenager.

Superman arrives at the lab and walks through the open doors. Inside, Lex Luthor sits waiting.

"Hello, Superman," Luthor says. "I was beginning to think you wouldn't make it. What a pity that would have been—for the people of Metropolis!"

Angrily, Superman strides over to the criminal genius, and lifts him up by his collar. "Careful, Superman," Luthor says confidently. "My computers can detect any injury to me and set off the Death Ray automatically!" Superman carefully sets Luthor back into the chair.

"That's better." Luthor smirks. "Now, I want *two* things that only you can get for me, Superman. The first is the youth serum possessed by the inhabitants of the Nexus solar system. They won't give it to *me*, but they would never turn down Earth's greatest hero!"

If Superman agrees to go on Luthor's mission, turn to page 105.

If Superman refuses to get the serum, turn to page 112.

Clark feels himself being lifted up and placed in a chair. Slowly, he opens his eyes.

"Ah, Mr. Kent, I'm glad you're awake," the evil mastermind named Lex Luthor says. "I want you to stay right here, so you can tell the readers of the *Daily Planet* how well Superman follows my every command.

"But his time is running out," Luthor chuckles. "If he doesn't arrive soon, you shall have no readers left in Metropolis!"

Clark knows he has to think quickly.

If Clark tries to escape, turn to page 14.

If Clark knocks Luthor out and changes into Superman, turn to page 103.

Soon the two are outside Lois' office. Lois swings open the door.

"TAA-DAA!" she shouts as she ushers Clark inside. The small office is almost totally filled up by an enormous cuckoo clock resting on the floor of the room. Ticking softly, the six-foot-wide wooden clock is a truly awesome sight.

"It's—er—beautiful, Lois," Clark says uncertainly. "But who sent it to you?"

"There was no card," Lois answers. "Hang on a moment, Clark—the clock is about to chime!"

Turn to page 54.

"Take six drops," Superman says.

Luthor opens the vial and greedily drinks the six drops. He watches in the mirror as the rejuvenation process begins.

First, the small wrinkles on his face disappear. Luthor grins joyfully. But as he looks down at his feet—his pants seem to be growing longer!

"What have you done!" he shouts at Superman, as he feels himself getting smaller and smaller. Superman says nothing, but continues to watch the amazing transformation.

Soon, where Lex once stood, a small infant plays happily on the floor. "Goo-goo," baby Lex says as Superman lifts him into his arms.

"I'll bring you to the Smallville Orphanage, Lex," Superman says. "Now you'll have a second chance to lead a good and honest life!"

The End

Slowly but surely, Clark edges to the door, hoping to escape Luthor so he can change into Superman and confront the fiend. But Luthor spots the reporter trying to make his getaway.

"So you refuse to cooperate?" Luthor says darkly. "Very well. I have a place for people like you!"

Luthor grabs the reporter by the collar and takes him down to the basement. There an underground sewer stretches for miles.

"Come along!" Luthor snarls. "I'm taking you to a place where no one will ever find you!"

(continued on page 15)

The two walk through the damp, dimly lit sewer for what seems like hours. Finally, Luthor stops to press a spot on the brick-lined walls. A secret door opens to reveal a room that looks like a prison cell.

"You'll rot here forever, Kent," Luthor says as he pushes Clark into the room and slams the door shut behind him.

"That's what *he* thinks," Clark whispers to himself as he listens to Luthor's steps fade in the distance.

When the sound of Luthor's footsteps is gone, Clark changes into the red, blue, and yellow costume of Superman!

The Man of Steel smashes through the wall, and bores up through the ground to the surface.

I'm clear on the other side of Smallville! Superman thinks. *I'd better fly over to Luthor's lab right away!*

Turn to page 9.

Superman dashes toward Lektor, but the Valgorian leader is too fast. He points the wand at Superman and Carnus, and black lightning shoots from its tip. In a flash, Superman and sorcerer are gone.

Moments later, Superman finds himself in a murky, twilight dimension. Nearby, Carnus sits sobbing.

"Where are we?" Superman asks.

"In the mystical dimension of Quil," the wizard answers.

"Is there a way out?" the Man of Steel asks.

"Yes," Carnus replies.

Superman brightens at the thought of escape. "How?" he asks.

"With the wand," Carnus groans.

"But Lektor has the wa–" Superman says.

"Correct," the wizard says. "So we must remain here—forever."

The End

I can't trust a device that has caused so much sorrow for the people of Valgor, Superman thinks. *I've got to destroy the wand— forever!*

Using all his strength, Superman throws the wand to the ground. When it hits, a blinding flash of light fills the throne room and bursts from the castle, covering the entire planet with its brilliance. In seconds, Valgor is magically transformed to its former majesty.

"The wand contained awesome power over Valgor," Superman declares. "By destroying it, I've saved a world!"

"Yes," King Vidus agrees. "And now that you have helped break the spell that Carnus placed on me, I can make peace. But first," Vidus says as he points to the beaten sorcerer, "GUARDS! Take Carnus away!"

The End

"Take two drops," Superman says.

Luthor quickly swallows the correct dosage. "Good! Good!" he shouts insanely. "I'll be young and strong forever! Already I feel the serum's effects!"

"And now," Lex says, regaining his composure, "for the second thing. I want you to take a trip with me, to a world with a red sun. There you will have no super powers, so I'll be able to fight you man-to-man and prove to the world that I am superior to you. I have reprogrammed my computer. The Death Ray will *not* go off if you injure me on the red sun planet, so we will be fighting as equals!"

If Superman agrees to go to the red sun planet, continue on page 19.

If Superman refuses to join Luthor on the red sun world, turn to page 104.

"Just let me program the computer to obey *my* verbal command to return us to Earth once the battle is over," Lex says, pressing some buttons on his computer terminal. "Good. Now let's go."

Luthor's Transporter Ray takes both hero and villain to a hazy desert world where a huge red ball of flame hangs in the sky. In three directions there is only desert as far as the eye can see, but in the west stands a huge range of craggy mountains.

If Superman remains in the desert and fights, turn to page 106.

If Superman flees to the mountains, turn to page 111.

Within minutes, Clark Kent is walking through the streets of Smallville—after flying to the small Midwestern town as Superman. Clark walks to the outskirts of town, to the laboratory once used by Lex Luthor.

Clark stands outside the open door. "Hello?" he asks. "Is anybody home?"

Getting no answer, Clark decides to go inside. But as soon as he steps through the doorway, he is hit on the head.

I'd better fake getting knocked out, Clark thinks, *or whoever hit me may become awfully suspicious.*

Clark slumps to the floor.

Turn to page 11.

In space, Superman catches up to the stunned monster. Its eyes seem soft and tearful, almost as if it were sad. Suddenly, the monster speaks in emotion-filled sobs.

"I am sorry for what I have done," the creature says, "but I was in pain, and lashed out unthinkingly. The Earth's atmosphere is too rich in oxygen for me. It made me delirious. I was not in control of myself."

Turn to page 22.

The creature continues:

"I come from the planet Valgor. My home world has been conquered by an evil and corrupt race of aliens. I escaped to seek the aid of Superman, the mightiest being in the universe. But I miscalculated the oxygen levels of your world and unintentionally caused some destruction. You must tell me—where can I find the one named Superman?"

"You're looking at him," Superman replies proudly.

"You?!" the creature says, astounded. "Then you must come back to Valgor with me—to save my world!"

Superman thinks for a moment. The yellow creature seems to be telling the truth. But it *could* be a trap. Only by using the lie detector in Superman's arctic Fortress of Solitude can he be certain that the monster is not lying.

If Superman takes the creature to the Fortress lie detector, turn to page 24.

If Superman goes directly to Valgor, turn to page 25.

Luthor lunges at Superman, punching him with all his strength. The Man of Steel winces in pain, but knows that he cannot fight back. To injure Lex would mean setting off the Death Ray aimed at Metropolis.

As blow after blow rains down on the ex-Man of Steel, Superman gets an idea. Slowly, he crawls toward the Transporter Ray in the center of the lab.

As Luthor approaches for the final blow, Superman clicks the Transporter on. The beam surrounds Luthor as he screams in panic.

"The computer is set for another galaxy! I'll be trapped there forever!" Lex shouts as he vanishes.

Still weak from the battle, Superman rises. He has beaten Lex Luthor, but the Gold Kryptonite has forever stripped him of his powers.

The End

Soon Superman and the creature from Valgor fly to the North Pole and arrive at the Fortress of Solitude. Superman sets the creature down at the door, and flies off to pick up the huge arrow-shaped direction marker that is also the key to the Fortress' door. Once the massive door is opened, the two enter.

"I'm sorry I have to do this," Superman says to the creature, "but I must be certain that you're telling the truth. The lie detector is this way. Follow me."

On the way, Superman and the alien creature pass a large doorway. Inside, in cages, are alien animals of all kinds.

The monster is fascinated by the interplanetary menagerie. "Superman," it asks, "can we take a moment to look over your alien zoo?"

If Superman agrees to tour the zoo, turn to page 34.

If Superman and the alien go directly to the lie detector, turn to page 29.

"All right, my friend," Superman says. "Let's go."

After covering the creature with his invulnerable cape, Superman takes off. In a blur of motion, he flies to the rim of the galaxy toward Valgor. In less than an hour, the two have arrived.

What Superman sees on the surface of the planet chills him. Valgor has been laid waste. Crumbling buildings are everywhere. There seems no sign of life. Howling winds blow unmercifully across the barren land.

From a distance, Superman can see a small group of alien creatures approaching.

"Who are they?" Superman asks.

"Friends," the creature assures him.

Turn to page 96.

Superman watches as a bolt of black lightning blasts from the wand, striking the helpless sorcerer. Then, with a pitiful cry, Carnus disappears.

"What have you done to him?" Superman asks Lektor, outraged.

"I have sent him to a dimension from which there is no escape," Lektor answers smugly.

Superman turns away in disgust, but Lektor continues to speak. "Do you realize the power of my wand, alien?" Lektor asks. "Join me, and together we shall rule the universe!"

Superman looks angrily at Lektor. "I shall never join you," he says. "You are as evil as poor Carnus!"

"Very well then," Lektor replies. "Since you now feel so sorry for the sorcerer, perhaps you would like to keep him company!"

Another bolt of black lightning spews out of the wand, hitting the Man of Steel. In an instant, Superman is gone—for all eternity!

The End

At super speed, the Man of Steel snatches the glowing wand from the wizard's hand and prepares to smash the wand to pieces. But suddenly, a mysterious voice calls out to him. Superman looks around, but sees no one talking. The voice is *inside* his head!

"I am the spirit of the Wand of Walmere," the voice says. "For eons, I have journeyed through the galaxy, serving one master after another. I have given them all riches beyond imagining, and I could do the same for *you*! Promise not to destroy me, and the universe can be yours!"

Superman considers the wand's offer. With its power at his command, he could easily restore Valgor to its former glory. Still, Superman is not certain.

If Superman accepts the wand's offer, turn to page 88.

If Superman rejects the wand's offer, turn to page 17.

Superman suddenly remembers his alien friend. "You must return the Phantom Zone criminals back to the Zone," he shouts, "before they destroy me!"

"But, Superman," the alien shouts back, "I don't know how the Zone projector works!"

"But *I* do!" the evil scientist named Kru-El says, as he swipes the alien aside, "and I'm going to *use* it on you two!"

Kru-El snatches the projector, focuses it on Superman and the alien, and turns the machine on.

Slowly, Superman and the alien feel their bodies begin to melt away, and before they know it, they have been reduced to phantoms, forever trapped in . . . the *Phantom Zone!*

The End

"Sorry, but *neither* of us has any time to waste," Superman says.

Superman and the alien step into the computer room, where the alien is seated in a futuristic computer chair.

In an instant, a computer printout reveals the lie detector's conclusions. The creature is telling the truth!

But as Superman reads the lie detector's results, he doesn't notice the creature as it rises from the chair and wanders among the Fortress' other complicated machines.

"Tell me, Superman—what does *this* machine do?" the creature asks as he presses a button on the Phantom Zone projector.

"NO!" Superman shouts. "Don't touch that!"

But it is too late.

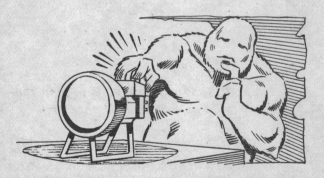

Turn to page 30.

"*Great Rao!*" Superman gasps, "the alien has freed the *Phantom Zone* villains!"

Superman watches, speechless, as three figures—each an infamous Kryptonian criminal sentenced to spend eternity in the Phantom Zone by Kryptonian judges—quickly materialize. In seconds, the three are completely solid. With their hands clenched into fists, they race to attack Superman!

If Superman attempts to fight the villains, continue on page 31.

If Superman evades the villains and rushes to turn off the Phantom Zone projector, turn to page 32.

The super-powered Kryptonian villains named General Zod, Kru-El, and Faora Hu-Ul approach the Man of Steel.

"So, Superman," General Zod says, "at last I shall have my revenge for being put into the Phantom Zone!"

As if in answer to Zod, Superman tenses his muscles for a super-punch—but it never hits the evil General! Instead, Kru-El and Faora dart behind the Man of Steel at super-speed, gripping him in a super-hammerlock!

Superman is totally helpless!

Turn to page 28.

At super-speed, the Man of Steel zigzags between the three fully materialized villains, grabs the Phantom Zone projector, and turns it off.

"And now," he says to General Zod, Kru-El, and Faora, "it's time to put *you* three back where you belong!" He aims the projector at the Phantom Zone escapees, but they flee the fortress in different directions.

"You alone are not strong enough to stop us, Superman," General Zod shouts back at the Man of Steel as he bursts through the Fortress' solid steel walls, "so we will conquer your planet and then return to destroy *you!*"

Left alone, Superman knows that he must act quickly.

Turn to page 38.

"Well," Superman says, "I guess it's okay."

Superman and the giant yellow creature enter the alien zoo. Amazing beasts collected from all over the universe are gathered there, from mini-dinosaurs to a singing butterfly from the star of Betelgeuse.

As the creature from Valgor walks among the glass cages, it passes by the giant insect-like Bravado Beast, who hates the color yellow. When the Bravado Beast sees the monster, it goes into a rage, smashing through its own cage and the cages nearby.

"Great Rao!" Superman says. "It's a stampede! We've got to stop them!"

The alien beasts charge into Superman's Kryptonite storage room. Just as Superman is about to corral the beasts, one of them knocks over a lead-lined glass showcase containing Kryptonite specimens. The glass shatters, exposing Superman to the deadly minerals.

"Help me!" Superman shouts to the creature.

"I can't!" the creature replies in terror. "The Bravado Beast has me in its clutches—and it won't let go!"

"Then this," Superman gasps, "is . . ."

The End

The communications monitors in the Fortress tell Superman that General Zod has fled to Washington, D.C., where he has kidnaped the President of the United States!

Within moments, Superman is flying over the White House. All around the President's home, tanks and soldiers stand ready to attack.

"What's going on here, Colonel?" the Man of Steel asks as he lands.

"We can't get close enough to find out many details," the Colonel answers, "but we *do* know that Zod demands to be made President! Looks like it's up to you, Superman—only you can save the country from that menace!"

"All right," the Man of Steel says calmly, readying himself. "I'm going in."

If Superman has . . .
  the Shrinking Ray, turn to page 48.
  the box of Red Kryptonite, turn to page 40.
  the Green Kryptonite Ray Gun, turn to page 44.

If Superman has no weapons, turn to page 41.

As Superman turns to his communications center to find out where the Phantom Zone criminal named Kru-El has gone, his super-hearing picks up a faraway distress signal.

"MAYDAY! MAYDAY! Metropolis Airlines Flight 29!" the voice says. "We've got some kinda super-powered creature out here, and he's tossin' our plane around the sky like it was made outta cotton candy! We can't stay airborne much longer! Superman, if you're listening, we need your help!"

In moments, Superman flies to the middle of the Atlantic Ocean. In the distance he sees Kru-El swinging the plane through the sky. "KRU-EL!" Superman shouts at the evil Kryptonian. "I'm coming for you!"

If Superman has . . .
the Shrinking Ray, turn to page 45.
the Green Kryptonite Ray Gun, turn to page 49.
The box of Red Kryptonite, turn to page 42.

If Superman has no weapons, turn to page 46.

Superman returns to his communications room to try to locate Faora. He switches on his international satellite monitor to see if anyone has sighted the female Phantom Zone criminal, but hears only static. After a short time, however, a female voice breaks through the noise.

"Hear me, Earthlings," the voice says. "I am Faora Hu-Ul—and I am Earth's DE-STROYER! I have reprogrammed all of Earth's satellites to fire deadly laser beams that will instantly atomize the entire planet! You are all finished!"

She's insane, Superman thinks. *Her only ambition is to destroy all of mankind—but I've got to stop her!*

Superman flies into space and, with his telescopic vision, locates the mad villainess.

If Superman has . . .

the Shrinking Ray, turn to page 47.

the box of Red Kryptonite, turn to page 43.

the Green Kryptonite Ray Gun, turn to page 50.

If Superman has no weapons, turn to page 51.

Superman races to the Fortress of Solitude's majestic Hall of Weapons, a veritable arsenal of exotic and otherworldly devices.

He gazes at a wall of weapons specifically designed to overpower super-powered menaces.

The first weapon is a Green Kryptonite Ray Gun, which fires a Kryptonite radiation beam that is deadly to any Kryptonian, including Superman.

The second weapon is a Shrinking Ray, which can reduce even the largest city to the size of an atom.

The third weapon is a box containing some chunks of Red Kryptonite—the type of Kryptonite that temporarily causes strange and unpredictable changes in the mind or body of any Kryptonian. Red Kryptonite can only affect a Kryptonian *once*, and Superman is already immune to these pieces.

Choose one of these weapons for Superman or let him go unarmed and turn to page 39.

The Man of Steel goes to the Fortress files to look for a hint to each villain's possible weakness.

(*You can see the Fortress files for yourself by turning to pages 117 and 118.*)

Superman examines the file cards on the three villains carefully. Then he decides which villain he must go after with his chosen weapon.

If Superman goes after . . .
General Zod, turn to page 35.
Kru-El, turn to page 36.
Faora, turn to page 37.

With the chunks of Red Kryptonite hidden inside a lead-lined box that X-ray vision cannot penetrate, Superman strides into the White House. Superman knows that the effects of Red Kryptonite are unpredictable, so he is uncertain of what to expect. Within moments he will find out.

He walks down the hall and finds General Zod sitting in the Oval Office. At first, Zod glares angrily at Superman, but when he sees the box the Man of Steel holds, he smiles. "How good of you to bring a housewarming gift for me," Zod says, "your new PRESIDENT!"

Zod grabs the box from Superman and opens it, revealing the glowing chunk of Red Kryptonite. His eyes open wide in disbelief as he groans and drops to the floor.

Moments later, the evil Kryptonian awakens. "Who—who am I?" he asks, confused. "And who are you? My, what a colorful costume you have. You must be a Super Hero!"

He's completely lost his memory! Superman thinks. *But that won't last long. The effect of Red Kryptonite wears off quickly, so I've got to get him back into the Phantom Zone before it does!*

Turn to page 52.

"Zod!" Superman shouts when he spots the villain. "You'll *never* take over this country— not as long as I'm around!"

"I can't beat you, Superman," Zod replies, an evil smile dawning on his lips, "but if you won't let me rule this country, then I'll DE- STROY the entire planet!"

In a blur of motion, Zod leaps straight for the ground. He bores through the floor and founda- tion of the White House, straight down into the red-hot molten core of the planet. There, he uses his super-strength to smash at the bub- bling cavern walls, causing huge earthquakes across the globe.

By the time Superman arrives to stop him, it is too late. Already a chain reaction has be- gun—one that will soon cause the whole world to explode!

"Say goodbye to Earth!" Zod proclaims mer- rily, and Superman knows he is right.

The End

"Go away, Superman!" Kru-El shouts. "I'm busy playing—leave me alone!"

Grimly, Superman opens the lead box and removes a chunk of Red Kryptonite. Superman knows that its effects are unpredictable, and crosses his fingers for luck. Then he speaks to Kru-El.

"Well, Kru-El—if you want to play, how about a game of catch!" Superman says as he hurls the red mineral at the brutish criminal.

Kru-El snatches the rock and stares at it curiously. In moments Superman notices that Kru-El's skin is turning *blue*—but the Red Kryptonite is having absolutely no other effect!

Soon Kru-El realizes what he has been holding. "Hey! This is KRYPTONITE!" he says. "You tried to *trick* me! But," he adds as he torpedoes the Kryptonite back at the Man of Steel, "it's not that easy to trick Kru-El!"

Superman catches the Red Kryptonite, places it back in the box, and takes off for the Fortress. He'll need a different weapon to trap THIS foe!

Turn to page 116.

The Man of Steel quickly sneaks up behind Faora, holding the lead-lined box of Red Kryptonite in his hand. *The effects of Red K are unpredictable,* he thinks, *but I've got to try to stop her!*

When the Man of Steel is in range of his enemy, he opens the box. The gleaming red rays shoot out, covering Faora. Soon the Kryptonian villainess begins to—GROW! Larger and larger she becomes, until the mighty Man of Steel is no bigger than a fly next to her!

"EARTH!" Faora roars angrily. "NOW I WILL DESTROY IT!" The villainess flies toward the planet, knowing that with each step she has greater power to destroy whole cities. Superman knows that he is powerless to stop her!

The End

As Superman enters the White House he sees the President tied to a chair at the top of the stairs. Superman rushes to release him, placing the Green Kryptonite Ray Gun on the floor. The evil General Zod is nowhere in sight.

"Mr. President," Superman says, "are you all right?"

"Yes, Superman," the President replies, "but—BEHIND YOU—LOOK OUT!"

But it is too late. Zod has crept up on the Man of Steel, knocking him out with a super-powered blow to his neck.

Moments later, when Superman awakens, he sees General Zod pointing the Kryptonite Ray Gun at him. "Ah, Superman," Zod snickers, "you have recovered. Good. I didn't want you to miss . . . THIS!"

Zod pulls the Ray Gun trigger and a beam of green radiation washes over the Man of Steel. Each second of exposure makes him weaker and weaker. Superman knows that this is . . .

The End

Superman holds the Shrinking Ray tightly in his hand and aims it at Kru-El. But when he cocks the trigger, the sound is heard by the Phantom Zone villain's keen super-hearing. With lightning-fast speed, Kru-El throws the airplane at the Man of Steel. The plane's wing glances off Superman's arm, and he drops the Shrinking Ray.

Before the Man of Steel can recover it, Kru-El swipes the weapon out of the sky and aims it at the Man of Steel.

"I've got you in my sights now, Superman—and I won't stop shrinking you until you're the size of the smallest atom! Goodbye, Man of Steel—have a nice trip!"

Superman feels a strange sensation as the wind seems to rush up around him. Soon boulder-like objects appear from out of nowhere. The Man of Steel realizes that these are, in fact, the very atoms that Kru-El spoke of, and that he will never be able to return to normal size again.

The End

At once, Superman is flying high over the Atlantic Ocean toward the kidnaped plane. There he sees Kru-El tossing the endangered aircraft about.

"Kru-El!" the Man of Steel shouts across the sky. "How about fighting ME?"

In seconds, the battle begins. The two super-powered Kryptonians exchange blow after blow, but, for sheet brute strength, Kru-El is stronger. With no weapons to help him, Superman feels himself growing weaker and weaker. He tries to flee, but Kru-El easily catches up with him. As the fight rages on, the Man of Steel hardly has enough strength to remain in the air. Soon, Superman realizes what the outcome of the struggle must be. He is doomed.

The End

Armed with his Shrinking Ray, Superman flies through space after the Phantom Zone villainess. When Faora sees him, the Man of Steel turns on the Shrinking Ray, bathing the Kryptonian criminal in its eerie white light. Faora feels herself getting smaller and smaller, and is powerless to stop the transformation!

"Curse you," she squeaks in a tiny voice as she dwindles away. With his microscopic vision Superman scans the sky and spots Faora—now no larger than the smallest insect! Snatching the miniaturized villainess out of space, Superman stashes her in his cape's hidden pouch and flies back to the Fortress.

Turn to page 52.

"Hold it, Zod!" Superman shouts as he walks into the White House. "I've got a surprise for you!"

The Man of Steel points the Shrinking Ray at the evil General and fires. But, using superspeed, Zod snatches the President, pushing *him* into the path of the ray beam.

"Oh, no!" the President groans. "I-I'm getting smaller every second! I-I'm SHRINK-ING!" Realizing his error, Superman reverses the ray's polarity, and the President soon returns to normal size.

"Sorry, Superman," Zod gloats, "but your shrinking device seems to have a *little* problem—so you'll never defeat me with it!"

Superman knows that Zod is right. *I'd better go back to the Fortress,* Superman thinks, *and find a better weapon to tackle this Phantom Zone criminal!*

Turn to page 116.

When Kru-El sees Superman, he releases the plane and rockets at him, but the Man of Steel holds his ground. Just as the monstrous Kryptonian is upon him, Superman fires the Green Kryptonite Ray Gun. Kru-El groans as the green ray begins to weaken him.

Feeling sorry for the Kryptonian criminal, Superman makes him an offer. "I'll turn off the ray," he says, "if you promise to come along quietly and allow me to return you to the Phantom Zone!"

"Anything! Anything!" Kru-El screams. "Just turn it off!"

Soon both hero and villain are flying back to the Fortress. On the way, Superman hears Kru-El mumbling to himself. "I never REALLY wanted to rule the Earth anyway," the Kryptonian criminal mutters.

Turn to page 52.

"Okay, Faora," Superman shouts as he points the Green Kryptonite Ray Gun at the villainess, "you're finished!"

In reply, Faora throws back her head and laughs. "So you think, Superman," she says. "So you think!"

Superman fires his Ray Gun, but, at super-speed, Faora flies to a nearby satellite and rips off its lead-lined reflective shield. The green beam hits the shield and bounces back at the Man of Steel, who winces in pain from the blast.

Again and again, Superman fires the Ray Gun, but each burst ricochets at him. Weakened, Superman soon flies away. *I've got to return to the Fortress for another weapon,* he thinks. *Before I really hurt myself!*

Turn to page 116.

When Superman finally reaches Faora, he is shocked. The villainess has gathered all of Earth's hundreds of orbiting satellites together, and has created a huge space maze with herself in the center.

"If you want me, Superman, you must maneuver through the satellite field first. But remember—touching a single satellite will activate my laser beams. One false move and Earth will be destroyed!"

Cautiously, Superman flies through the satellite mine field. He is almost upon Faora when the Kryptonian criminal flashes an evil smile. "So you think you've caught me fair and square, eh, Superman?" she grins. "Well, guess again! You see—I CHEAT!"

With that, Faora uses her super-breath to blow a gust of wind at Superman. The Man of Steel reels backward, landing on one of the satellites.

Dazed, Superman looks down upon Earth. A dozen ruby-red beams tear through space toward the planet's surface. Faora has won—the Earth is doomed.

The End

Moments later, Superman arrives at the Fortress, immediately turns on the Phantom Zone projector, and watches as his enemy slowly dematerializes. Soon, the Kryptonian foe is gone.

If Superman still has other Phantom Zone villains to capture, turn to page 116 to prepare for battle.

If he has now returned all the villains to the Phantom Zone, continue on page 53.

"Well, that's it!" Superman says. "All the Kryptonian criminals have been returned to the Phantom Zone. I hope they never escape again.

"Now, my friend," Superman continues, "it's time for us to free the citizens of Valgor and—" Superman turns to face the creature but it is gone. "Where has it gone *now?*" the Man of Steel wonders.

"Superman!" the creature shouts from the other end of the room. "I'm over here!" It is looking at yet another piece of the Fortress' complicated machinery. "Tell me, Superman," the creature asks as it prepares to touch the machine. "What does *this* do?"

"Oh no!" Superman groans. "Not again!"

The Man of Steel races to the creature and lifts it into the air. "You've caused enough trouble for one day!" he says sternly. "Come on. We're off to Valgor."

Turn to page 25.

At the stroke of one, the enormous cuckoo clock begins to chime. Slowly, the huge door above the dial creaks open. Inside, all is black, except for a pair of shining green eyes peering out.

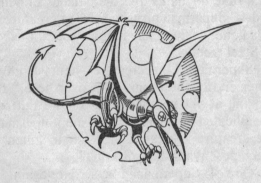

Suddenly, a huge robot bird shoots out of the doorway. It hovers over the room for a moment, as if searching out its prey, then swoops down, grabs Lois with its sharp metal claws, and streaks out the window!

Great Krypton! Clark thinks. *I've got to save Lois! But the clock is still ticking—it might be a bomb!*

If Clark switches to Superman and goes after Lois, continue on page 55.

If Clark examines the clock to see if it is a bomb, turn to page 57.

In seconds, Clark changes into Superman and is off. Soon he has caught up with the giant metal bird creature, with Lois struggling in its claws.

"SUPERMAN!" she says when she spies the blue, red, and yellow costume. "Thank heaven you showed up!"

"Hang on, Lois," Superman answers. "I'll have this cagey bird caged again in a second!"

At that moment, the metal bird turns toward its adversary, opens its eyes, and two green rays stream out.

KRYPTONITE! Superman thinks. *Its eyes are made of Kryptonite, making me weak! I— I've got to get away!*

Stunned by the lethal rays, the Man of Steel plummets to Earth.

Turn to page 56.

Down, down the Man of Tomorrow falls toward the city below. Superman's strength begins to return mere seconds before crashing into the heart of midtown Metropolis, and once again he is aloft.

Suddenly, the sound of an explosion fills the air, and Superman quickly turns in the direction of the noise.

Clouds of black smoke billow out of Lois Lane's office at the *Daily Planet* building. *Great Krypton!* Superman thinks. *The clock was a bomb! I only hope that no one was hurt!*

In a flash, Superman is in Lois' smoke-filled office.

"We're all right, Superman," photographer Jimmy Olsen says. "But this office is a mess! I guess the only thing to do is clean up! Want to help?"

If Superman decides to help clean up, turn to page 58.

If Superman decides to go after Lois again, turn to page 59.

Clark uses his X-ray vision to look inside the clock. Sure enough, a powerful bomb is planted deep inside. As Lois and her mechanical kidnaper disappear over the horizon, Clark uses his heat vision to sever the bomb's wires. Next to the wires, Clark spots a clue.

"Hmm . . ." he says. "Those are tickets to today's Ultimate Videogame Tournament! I wonder if that has anything to do with Lois' kidnaping? I think Superman ought to check it out!"

Turn to page 64.

"All right, Jimmy," Superman says. "I'll have the job done in a second. Just stand back."

Moving to the center of the smoke-filled room, Superman inhales deeply. His super-lungs suck the smoke out of the office, cleaning it completely. Then the Man of Steel steps to the window and exhales, sending gusts of smoke into the air.

"WOW!" Jimmy gasps. "What a guy!"

Superman uses his telescopic vision to scan the debris in Lois' office, hoping to find a clue. Next to the cuckoo clock's charred remains, Superman sees a pair of tickets for today's Ultimate Videogame Tournament, at the Metropolis Coliseum.

I've got a hunch I'll find Lois there, Superman thinks as he flies off.

Turn to page 64.

"Sorry, Jimmy," Superman answers. "You'll have to do that yourself! I've got to save Lois—she's in *real* trouble!"

The Man of Steel scans the sky, but the mechanical bird and its captive have escaped.

Hmmm . . . Superman thinks. *I know that Lois was working on a dangerous assignment to expose a certain dishonest toy manufacturer. Whoever kidnaped her might not want her story to appear. Perhaps I should use my telescopic vision to consult the fact file at the Fortress of Solitude—it might help me figure out which villain is behind all this.*

You can look at Superman's Fortress file by turning to page 117.

Then turn to page 60.

Superman stands outside an old toy factory on the outskirts of Metropolis. Over the huge wooden door is a sign that reads:

TOYMEISTER TOYS:
HOME OF THE SUPERMAN FUN LINE!

The door is ajar, so Superman enters.

Inside, people are working busily, putting the finishing touches on the newest Toymeister toy. They are so occupied with their work that they do not notice the Man of Steel.

Near Superman, three workers tip over a huge vat of molten lead, carefully pouring the liquid metal into tiny molds.

Superman decides to take a closer look at the toys that the workers are making. They are little Superman dolls!

"Ah, Superman," a voice suddenly calls out. "I'm so glad you've come!"

Superman turns to confront the voice—it's the TOYMAN!

If Superman attempts to capture the Toyman, turn to page 62.

If he waits for the Toyman to make the next move, turn to page 63.

Superman lunges at the Toyman—and passes right *through* the criminal mastermind!

"Surely you don't expect me to confront you in person?" the Toyman gloats. "This is merely a hologram of myself!"

"Where is Lois?" Superman shouts at the image.

"She is safe," the Toyman replies. "But *you* are not."

The Toyman opens his hand to reveal a small radio controller. He turns the dial slowly. The workers behind Superman stop their activities and look ahead blankly. Shocked, Superman suddenly realizes that the workers are not human at all—they're robots!

Then the toys that the robot workers were making begin to move. Over a thousand Superman dolls stand ready to obey the Toyman's next command!

Turn to page 114.

Superman watches as the Toyman turns a dial on the radio controller in his hand. Suddenly, the mini-Superman dolls on the factory tables stand up and begin to fly at Superman! Even at a distance, Superman can see their Green Kryptonite eyes flickering menacingly.

Thinking quickly, Superman reaches for the huge vat of lead next to him. He lifts it over his head and tosses its contents at the pack of rapidly approaching deadly dolls. The molten lead covers the pack of dolls, stopping them in their tracks. As one, they fall to the floor in a bubbling heap.

The lead should shield me from their Kryptonite eyes, Superman thinks. *And now, I'd better get the Toyman!*

But the villain has vanished. Near where he stood are two hallways. One is dark and silent. From the other, Superman hears the voice of Jimmy Olsen calling for help!

If Superman rescues Jimmy, turn to page 83.

If Superman enters the other hall to search for Lois, turn to page 109.

Soon Superman is at the Metropolis Coliseum, where the Ultimate Videogame Championship is in progress. All around him are the two most popular videogames—Intergalactic Mutants and Maze Master. Each machine is being played by a contestant.

No sign of Lois here, Superman thinks. But then, something catches his eye. In a corner of the Coliseum is a door with the words "Private—Do Not Enter" over it. Jutting out from the bottom of the door is a notebook—with the name "Lois Lane" written on it!

Whatever's going on in there may be private, Superman thinks, *but if it concerns Lois, it concerns me!*

Superman opens the door and enters. Inside, a huge computer monitors the videogame activity outside. And in front of the computer console sits none other than—the terrible Toyman!

(continued on page 65)

"Ah, Superman," the Toyman snickers. "I've been expecting you! You've come in search of Ms. Lane, no doubt. She's right over there," he says, pointing to a computer chair in the corner of the room. "But I'm afraid that she's rather indisposed right now!"

Superman walks over to the computer chair where Lois is seated. She appears to be sleeping.

"You fiend!" Superman shouts angrily. "What have you done to her?"

"Her consciousness is now *inside* one of my two videogames," the Toyman chuckles. "She will stay there until *you* rescue her—or die trying! Just remember, Man of Steel, that inside the videogame you will have no super powers. Now, which game do you choose?"

If Superman decides to play Intergalactic Mutants, turn to page 66.

If Superman decides to play Maze Master, turn to page 74.

If Superman decides not to play any games, turn to page 81.

"I choose Intergalactic Mutants," Superman says as he sits down in the empty computer chair next to Lois.

"Very well, Superman," the Toyman says as he presses a button on the computer console. "Have a nice trip!"

The room seems to darken, and Superman suddenly finds himself holding a deadly laser blaster on a strange lunar surface. Above him, a huge spaceship glows brightly as ugly alien forms begin to drop out of it. Each alien holds a laser gun. Suddenly, one of them fires.

The laser beam rips through the sky, glancing off the Man of Steel.

"Ouch!" Superman shouts in pain. "The Toyman was right—I really don't have any super powers here, so I'd better defend myself! But the aliens are almost upon me—I've only got time for one shot!"

If Superman tries to blast the advancing aliens, turn to page 68.

If Superman tries to blast the spaceship, turn to page 113.

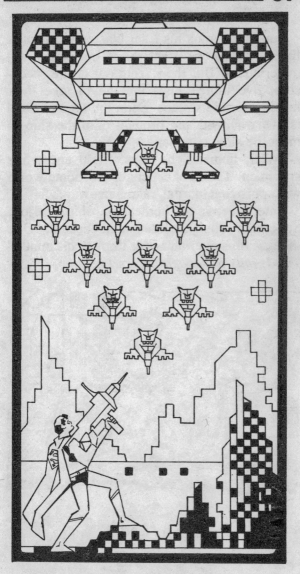

Superman aims his laser blaster and fires at the closest alien. It shrieks in horror and dematerializes. But then, from out of the spaceship, five more aliens emerge to take their fallen comrade's place. Soon the Man of Steel is overwhelmed and brought onto the ship to meet the alien commander.

"Well, human," he says. "You are a fine specimen. The zookeepers of our home world will approve. Guards! Take him away!"

Later, deep in the homebound ship's prison, Superman sits shackled and beaten. One thought runs over and over through his mind—*This is only a videogame, isn't it?!*

The End

Superman fires the force field generator at the nearest android, surrounding the robot warrior with an invisible shield. Sensing the danger, the android fires its laser gun. But the shield forces the laser beam back at the android, causing the robot to explode on contact.

Superman continues to fire the force field at the mindless androids, and one by one they are destroyed by their own weapons. Soon bubbling, smoldering heaps of metal debris are all that remain of the android threat.

Minutes later, Superman approaches the transporter tube. Stepping inside, the Man of Steel vanishes instantly.

Turn to page 94.

I have only fifteen seconds' worth of energy, Superman thinks. *I've got to make each second count!*

Superman turns on the force field generator and covers himself with its invisible shield. He steps on the glowing walkway and begins running toward the transporter tube at the end. The androids fire their guns, but their laser beams bounce harmlessly off the transparent force field.

The barrage continues as the seconds tick by. 9—8—7—6—

It's farther away than I thought! Superman thinks.

5—4—3—

I-I'm not going to make it!

2—1—0! The force field melts away. It is—

The End

"Here goes nothing!" Superman says as he presses the hyperdrive button. Suddenly, the ship disappears—only to reappear directly in front of a huge, oncoming meteor!

Superman tries to maneuver out of the way, but it is too late. The meteor plows into the small space fighter, smashing it to bits. Floating helplessly in space, the Man of Steel knows this is . . .

The End

As the ship streaks through space, Superman pushes the photon torpedo button, and watches in awe as the meteors explode into fragments. Soon he reaches the floating castle. With a single well-placed blast, Superman shatters the huge steel doors and lands the ship inside.

"Well done, Superman," the voice of the Toyman suddenly booms. "You have actually *won* your game of Intergalactic Mutants! Only a true champion could do that!

"However," the Toyman continues, "it is my sad duty to inform you that you have chosen the *wrong* game to play if you wanted to find Ms. Lane! But if you're willing, an *extra*-challenging game of Maze Master can be arranged!"

If Superman agrees to play Maze Master, turn to page 74.

If Superman decides not to play any more of the Toyman's games, turn to page 102.

Suddenly, a gust of super-breath hits the sorcerer's magic scepter, knocking it from his hand and out the palace window. The wizard can only watch helplessly as it flies off into space. "My wand," Carnus moans softly. "Without it, I'm powerless!"

Moments later, Superman watches silently as King Vidus, in control once again, passes judgment upon the traitorous Carnus. "You sought to control me and, through me, my people," he says sternly. "For that crime, you shall spend the rest of your days in prison!"

As the evil sorcerer is led off by the Paralyte guards, the king turns to Superman. "I am sorry for what has happened," Vidus says. "But now, I shall work with the Valgorians to rebuild their once-proud kingdom. Together, we shall prosper for all eternity."

The Man of Steel smiles. He knows that King Vidus is right.

The End

"Okay, Toyman," Superman says. "You've got me in a bind. I'll play Maze Master."

No sooner has Superman uttered his choice, than he is instantly transported to the strange, maze-like arena of the computer game. From around a corner four furry monsters appear. Looking extremely hungry, they begin to chase the Man of Steel.

Superman flees as fast as he can, but the monsters are tricky and try to corner the powerless Man of Steel in the maze.

In desperation, Superman crawls up the side of one of the maze walls. From the top, he can see the entire maze. In the center is an arrow that points to a large glowing disc. Along two of the walls are doorways that lead into dark tunnels.

Superman also sees the monsters approaching. He cannot stay on top of the maze wall any longer.

If Superman runs toward the glowing disc, turn to page 101.

If Superman heads for one of the doorways, turn to page 107.

Superman fires the blaster at the giant worm.
The insect groans as it feels the effects of the
ray gun. Soon it drops to the cavern floor. In
disgust, Superman turns away and looks for a
way out of the tunnel.

But then a weak, slippery voice speaks.

"No way out," the huge worm groans.

Superman is stunned. "Y-you can speak!"

"Yes . . ." the creature replies. "And only I
could have dug you a path out of here. But now
I am weak, too weak to go on. And without
me," the worm gasps, "you will be trapped
here forever!"

The End

I made a terrible mistake by giving Lektor the wand, Superman thinks as he rushes at the alien leader. *I only hope it's not too late to correct my error!*

Superman flies between Lektor and Carnus, hoping to shield the evil sorcerer from the wand's power.

"Wait, Lektor!" Superman pleads. "Don't destroy Carnus!"

"Why should I spare *his* life?" Lektor says as a crowd of Valgorian rebels gather nearby. "He would have destroyed us!"

Suddenly, Superman sees his chance.

If Superman tries to reason with Lektor, turn to page 91.

If Superman tries to overpower Lektor, turn to page 16.

"No," Superman says. "The power of the wand is too great for *any* creature to control. It must be destroyed."

With a swing of his mighty arm, Superman tosses the wand high into space, sending it hurtling into the heart of a distant sun.

Soon, Carnus and the Paralyte warriors arrive to reclaim the stolen wand. "Where is it?" Carnus stammers angrily. "Give it back to me!"

"You're too late, Carnus," Superman answers. "The wand is gone, and without it you are powerless. Now you and your people must leave Valgor forever, or face the wrath of its people." Knowing they are beaten, the Paralytes flee.

Soon, with Superman's help, the Valgorians begin rebuilding their ravaged world. "It will take much time and work," Superman tells Lektor, "but one day, Valgor will be beautiful again."

With tears of happiness in his eyes, Lektor agrees.

The End

Superman runs down one of the tunnels as he flees from the worm creature. Suddenly, the worm speaks.

"STOP!" it says. "That is not the way to freedom! Let me help you!"

Superman is stunned. "What—who are you?" he asks.

"I am the Tunnel Master," the worm answers. "I will help you find the one you seek."

In moments, the worm has dug an escape tunnel for the Man of Steel. "The one you search for is up there," the worm says as he leads Superman to the foot of a tall skyscraper that stands in a clearing near the tunnel. The worm quickly returns to the hole, leaving Superman alone once again.

"Now how am I going to get to the roof?" Superman wonders.

If Superman tries to crawl up the side of the building, turn to page 108.

If Superman walks inside the skyscraper to find a way to the roof, turn to page 95.

With a single sweep of his mighty arms, Superman scatters the guards that surround him, and heads toward the king and his wizard.

"You see?" Carnus says. "I told you so! He is evil, and must be dispatched before he destroys us!"

"Yes, Carnus, you are right," Vidus says as he slips back into his trance-like state. "Do what you must."

Carnus raises his wand high into the air as bolts of black lightning spew out of its tip, surrounding the Man of Steel.

My powers cannot protect me from the effects of magic, Superman thinks as the bolts whirl around him. *What is Carnus doing to me?*

Soon, Superman has his answer. Carnus has magically transported him to a strange, alien dimension—from which there can be no escape!

The End

Superman climbs to the top of the skyscraper's water tower and shouts at the huge gorilla. In anger, the gigantic ape tosses a girder at Superman, but misses, hitting the water tower instead.

A tremendous explosion rocks the building, and Superman and Lois are instantly transported back to the Toyman's computer room. Immediately, the Man of Steel slices through the computer with his heat vision, and grabs the fleeing Toyman.

"Are you okay?" Superman asks a still groggy Lois.

"I'm fine, Superman," Lois answers. "But I'm never playing a videogame again!"

The End

"I'm not in the mood for games today," Superman says as he uses his heat vision to slice through the Toyman's computer console. Sparks fly across the room as the computer sputters to a halt.

From the corner of his eye, Superman sees the Toyman trying to escape.

"Not so fast, Toyman," Superman says as he grabs the criminal genius by the collar. "You're going to prison—*after* you get Lois' mind out of the computer!"

"I-I can't!" the Toyman groans. "You destroyed the master computer! She's trapped in there—and there's no way out!"

Superman knows the Toyman is right. He has failed, and Lois is lost—forever!

The End

"I have a confession to make," the Clark robot says. "I am a robot! But the Toyman made me an *exact* duplicate of the real Clark Kent—so I care for Lois as much as *he* does, and wouldn't want anything bad to happen to her. You must believe me! She's down the hall—save her now!

Superman is touched by the robot's plea. "All right. I'll save her," he agrees.

The Man of Steel turns to leave. As he does, the Clark robot's eyes glow green. Twin beams of Kryptonite stream out, hitting the Man of Steel squarely in the back. He drops to the floor in agony.

"Fool," the robot says as the beams batter the Man of Steel into unconsciousness. "Never trust the Toyman's robots!"

The End

He's kidnaped Jimmy Olsen too! Superman thinks. *I've got to save him!*

As Superman follows the sound of Jimmy's voice, he wonders how the evil Toyman could have kidnaped the young photographer. But there is little time to think. Soon the Man of Steel enters the room where Jimmy has been tied up.

"Superman!" Jimmy shouts happily. "Untie me quickly before the Toyman comes back!"

The Man of Steel looks deep into Jimmy's eyes. *No Kryptonite there,* he thinks.

If Superman unties Jimmy, turn to page 100.

If Superman examines Jimmy more closely, turn to page 84.

"Just a second, Jimmy," Superman says. "I'd like to examine you a bit more before I untie you."

With his X-ray vision Superman looks deep inside Jimmy's body. But instead of seeing flesh and blood, the Man of Steel sees only gears, levers, and computer circuitry!

"Toyman!" Superman shouts angrily. "I know you can hear me! I'm coming for you!"

Suddenly the Jimmy robot begins to talk. "My master is too smart for you, Superman. Ms. Lane is in the very next room—but you will never save her!"

"We'll see about that," Superman says.

Turn to page 87.

Superman gives the wand to the rebel leader. Lektor's eyes gleam with mad joy as he snatches the wand from Superman's outstretched hand.

"First," Lektor says, "I shall restore our home world to its former glory!" Lektor swings the wand high over his head, and in a flash Valgor is once again whole. Gleaming golden-spired towers rise up from the ashen ground. A brilliant, warming sun appears in the sky. The sound of birds fills the air.

Lektor smiles shrewdly. "And now," he announces, "the time has come—for REVENGE!"

Lektor swings the wand once again and, as if from nowhere, Carnus appears. The evil sorcerer quakes in fear. "P-please," he begs. "Do not hurt me!"

Superman sees the look of undisguised hate in Lektor's eyes as he begins to swing the wand a final time.

If Superman prevents Lektor from harming Carnus, turn to page 76.

If Superman lets Lektor get his revenge, turn to page 26.

"Wait!" Superman shouts at the king. "Carnus is the evil one! It is *he* who thrives on war and destruction! I ask only for peace!"

"He lies, I tell you!" Carnus insists as he frantically waves his wand in the air.

King Vidus seems caught between the choices that Superman and Carnus offer. He looks dazed, as if rudely awoken from a long sleep. But as Superman and the magician continue to exchange words, the Paralyte king's eyes flicker with the light of reason.

"Guards!" he orders. "Return to your posts. I wish to speak further with the alien."

Knowing he has lost the battle of words, Carnus flies into a rage. "Somehow you have overcome the hypnotic spell I placed on you to do my bidding!" he screams at Vidus. "So now you are of no further use to me! Farewell, Vidus!"

The wizard waves his wand in the air as he turns his back on Superman. *He's going to do something horrible to Vidus,* Superman thinks. *I've got to stop him!*

If Superman grabs the wand from the wizard's hand, turn to page 27.

If Superman uses a gust of superbreath to blow the wand away, turn to page 73.

With a burst of heat vision, Superman destroys the robot and runs down the hall to the next room. There he sees two lead-lined doors with video screens above each. The screens show images of two Lois Lanes. A vanishing ray is focused on each figure.

Suddenly, the voice of the Toyman is heard. "I'm very proud of my robots, Superman, so proud I'm willing to bet that without your X-ray vision you can't tell the difference between the real Lois and the Lois robot! As soon as you open one door, both rays will fire! You will only have time to save one of them! Decide which one is Lois—NOW!"

Superman looks closely at the two video images. On the screen above the first door, Lois' green eyes flash defiantly. On the screen above the second, Lois stands bravely. Suddenly, Superman's choice is clear.

If Superman chooses door number one, turn to page 99.

If Superman chooses door number two, turn to page 110.

"All right," Superman says. "I accept."

"Good," the voice inside his head replies. "And now for your reward."

Suddenly, bolts of pain shoot through the Man of Steel's brain, knocking him unconscious. When he awakens, he is sitting on King Vidus' throne, unable to move or speak.

Soon the wizard Carnus approaches. In one hand he holds King Vidus' crown. In the other, he holds the magic wand.

"The wand always delivers what it promises," Carnus chuckles. "You *shall* have riches beyond imagining," he says as he places the crown on Superman's head, "but, under my magical powers, you shall serve *me* as a puppet king—forever!"

Unable to reply, Superman knows that he is beaten.

The End

Late that evening, Superman silently enters the evil wizard's chamber. He glides past the sleeping sorcerer and quickly finds the box containing the magic wand. As he touches the box, magical energy bolts burn the Man of Steel's hands.

He's placed a spell on the box! Superman thinks in agony. *And I'm not immune to the effects of magic! It hurts, but I've got to resist the pain and get the wand—for the people of Valgor!*

Resisting the impulse to cry out, Superman opens the box and snatches the wand. Suddenly, the pain fades. The spell is broken—and Carnus still sleeps soundly!

Superman flies from the Paralyte castle. As he returns to the rebel base, he is greeted by Lektor.

"Have you succeeded?" Lektor asks suspiciously.

"Yes," Superman replies.

"Good. The wand—give it to me."

If Superman gives Lektor the wand, turn to page 85.

If Superman destroys the wand, turn to page 77.

The boulder crashes into the villain, knocking him off the side of the mountain, onto the desert sands below.

From the mountaintop, Superman can see that his enemy has been mortally wounded. He rushes down to confront the criminal mastermind.

"I've beaten you, Luthor," Superman says solemnly.

"Perhaps," Luthor answers weakly. "But it was not a fair fight. Without my voice command to return us to Earth, you will spend the rest of your life here, powerless." Luthor gasps a final time and is silent.

Superman knows he did not make the best choice.

The End

"Lektor!" Superman continues. "To destroy Carnus would make you as evil as he! Is that what you want?"

"Yes!" Lektor replies. "I will crush him, and *all* those who stand in my way! Finally, I have the power!"

As Lektor continues, the noble Valgorian rebels hear his mad ravings. For a moment, they whisper among themselves. "The wand's power has made Lektor insane," they say. "We must stop him!"

Then, as one, the Valgorians descend on their leader, swarming over him before the wand can do its evil work.

Superman sees the wand fall to the ground and, with his heat vision, burns it to a crisp.

With the wand destroyed, Lektor seems to come out of a trance. "The wand was controlling my actions," he says. "Its power was too great. But now that it is gone, we shall try to make peace with the Paralytes."

Superman knows that Lektor will do his best.

The End

"Okay, Lektor," Superman says. "I'll help you. What's the plan?"

Lektor smiles slyly as he reveals his scheme to the Man of Steel. "You must fly to the capital this evening and enter the wizard Carnus' chambers. Our spies have told us that each night he places his magic scepter in a small box near his bed. You must steal the wand, for without it Carnus is powerless. Return here with the wand and give it to me. That alone will turn the tide of our struggle!"

Turn to page 89.

Instantly, the Man of Steel is transported to the end of a long, dark corridor. A glowing yellow walkway leads the way to a transporter tube far off in the distance.

"Enemy alert. Destroy intruder," a cold, mechanical voice calls out, as six heavily armed androids step from the shadows and onto the glowing path, blocking Superman's way. Then the voice of the Toyman speaks again:

"Now you must avoid the deadly computer androids and get to the transporter tube. Your only defense is the force field generator you will find on the ground—and it has only enough energy for fifteen seconds of use."

If Superman fires the force field at the androids, turn to page 69.

If Superman surrounds himself with the force field and races to the transporter, turn to page 70.

Whoosh! The tube lifts the Man of Steel high into the sky, transporting him to the controls of a speeding space fighter. Outside, huge meteors career through space, some heading straight for the ship!

Beyond the meteor belt, Superman can see a beautiful castle floating in space. Superman knows that this is his destination. But how can he get safely past the meteors?

The speeding spacecraft has only two controls, a button marked "Photon Blasters" and another marked "Hyperdrive."

If Superman maneuvers and blasts through the meteor field, turn to page 72.

If Superman presses the Hyperdrive button, turn to page 71.

Inside the skyscraper's lobby, Superman finds an elevator. *How convenient*, he thinks as he rides to the 100th floor.

On the roof, Superman finds the reason for his quest—LOIS LANE! But she is guarded by a huge ferocious gorilla! When the ape sees Superman, it goes mad, throwing bricks and girders at him. Superman avoids the barrage, as Lois shouts a warning to him:

"You've got to stop the Toyman! He's planning to use his videogame computer to take over the minds of all the contestants in his tournament! I found out about his scheme so he kidnaped me! The computer's master memory is hidden in that water tower! You've got to destroy it!"

Turn to page 80.

Soon the group of aliens meet the Man of Steel.

"We are the rebels of Valgor," the oldest-looking alien says. "I am Lektor, their leader."

"What has happened here?" Superman asks, outraged by the destruction around him.

"What you see is the work of the Paralytes," Lektor says mournfully. "They have enslaved our people and have taken over our capital city, living off the wealth we worked so hard to create.

"Their leader, King Vidus, is an evil creature. But Carnus, his wizard, is much worse. Some say that it is he, not the king, who is in control."

"You must try to reason with them," Superman says.

"NO!" Lektor shouts angrily. "The time for peace is past! Now is the time for war! With you at our side, we shall rid Valgor of the Paralytes forever!"

If Superman joins the rebels in their fight, turn to page 92.

If Superman tries to make peace with the Paralytes, turn to page 98.

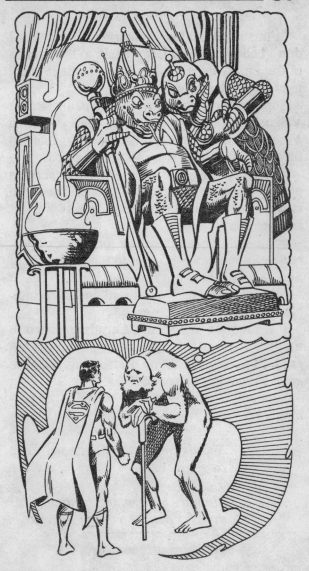

"I'm sorry, Lektor," Superman says, "but I don't believe in war. Let me talk to the leaders of the Paralytes. Perhaps I can convince them to change their ways."

Superman flies off, arriving moments later at Valgor's capital to make his plea to King Vidus. Soon he enters the heavily guarded throne room where King Vidus is seated.

"King Vidus, I implore you," Superman pleads, "choose the path of peace. Then you can live alongside the noble people of Valgor, and prosper together!"

King Vidus has a faraway look in his eyes, but as Superman continues to talk, the Man of Steel's words begin to ring true.

"Yes," Vidus says, confused and uncertain. "Perhaps there *can* be peace."

Just then the evil wizard Carnus storms into the throne room. "King Vidus!" he shouts angrily. "I demand that you destroy this creature *now!* He cannot be trusted!"

Suddenly, armed guards surround Superman.

Should Superman fight now? Turn to page 79.

Should Superman continue his plea for peace? Turn to page 86.

Superman dashes through the door and, at super-speed, smashes the vanishing ray.

"Lois!" the Man of Steel asks. "Are you all right?"

The figure hesitates a moment before answering. "Yes," she finally answers. "All circuits are functional."

The Man of Steel gasps in horror. He may capture the Toyman, but he will never see Lois again!

The End

In an instant, Superman unties the cub photographer.

"And now I've got to find Lois," the Man of Steel says.

"Wait a second, Superman," Jimmy calls out. "I'd like a picture for the front page of the next edition."

"Why, er, sure, Jimmy," Superman answers, "but make it snappy, okay?"

"Say cheese," Jimmy says as he aims the camera.

Superman smiles, but his grin quickly fades. A beam of Kryptonite comes out of the camera lens, knocking him to the ground.

"You—you're a robot!" Superman gasps.

"Yes," the robot Jimmy answers. "And you're about to become one *ex*-Superman! Goodbye, 'Pal'!"

The End

Superman charges the center of the maze. When he reaches the disc, he discovers that underneath it is a tunnel leading underground! With the monsters quickly approaching, Superman hops into the opening, and slides the cover back over the hole.

As Superman walks along the subterranean path, he finds a strange blaster gun that he takes along with him. Soon he comes to a fork in the dark cavern trail.

As the Man of Steel tries to decide which path to take, he hears a shuffling sound behind him. Turning, he sees a huge, slimy worm-like creature slithering toward him, its mouth dripping with green slime as if hungry for food!

If Superman destroys the worm with his blaster, turn to page 75.

If Superman flees down one of the tunnels, turn to page 78.

"No way!" Superman shouts angrily. "I'm getting out—right now!"

But just then, Superman feels his body vanishing. Unable to move, he can only listen as the Toyman begins to rant and rave:

"Have it your way, Superman, but I'm afraid I can't allow you to leave the computer. Instead, you will become a part of my greatest computer challenge—the Superman Video Game! Every time someone decides to play, you will be forced to fight! And someday, Man of Steel, you will LOSE!"

As he feels himself being transported directly into the computer's main memory banks, Superman realizes that the Toyman has won!

The End

Perhaps a little heat vision will do the trick! Clark thinks as he severs the wires holding a lamp above Luthor's head. The lamp drops on the bald scientist's head, knocking him out.

Moments later, when Luthor awakens, he is staring at the red, blue, and yellow costume of Superman!

"Okay, Lex," Superman says. "Funtime is over!"

"You fool!" Lex shouts in terror. "When you injured me, my computer automatically set off the Death Ray—Metropolis has already been destroyed!"

Using his telescopic vision, Superman sees that Lex is telling the truth!

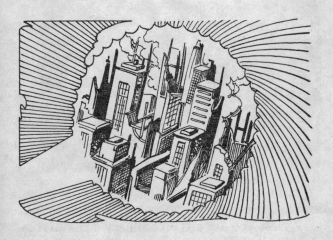

The End

"Lex, *I'm* not going anywhere!" Superman says.

"So you refuse a fair battle?" Luthor says angrily. "Very well then—we shall have our fight right here!" Without warning, Luthor opens a lead-lined box on his lab table and produces a glowing yellow chunk of Gold Kryptonite! He throws it at the Man of Steel, who cowers in fear as he is covered by its rays.

"Exposure to *Gold* Kryptonite will take away your superpowers forever!" Luthor cackles. "Now you are just an ordinary man—and I shall finally be able to crush you!"

Turn to page 23.

At the speed of light, Superman soars through space toward the planet Maitor in the Nexus solar system. Soon he arrives on the planet, and is met by a group of ambassadors.

"Hail to Superman, Champion of Earth," the leader of the delegation says. "Your exploits are legend throughout the galaxy. To what do we owe the honor of this visit?"

"I'm looking for the serum of Eternal Youth," the Man of Steel answers.

"Surely," the leader says, producing a vial from his pocket. "Here it is—but remember, never take more than two drops, or terrible things may happen."

"Thanks," Superman says as he flies away. "I'll remember that!"

Soon Superman returns to Luthor's lab. "Here's your serum, Luthor," Superman says.

"Thanks," Luthor cackles. "But tell me, Superman—how much should I take?"

If Superman tells Luthor the right amount, turn to page 18.

If Superman tells Luthor the wrong amount, turn to page 13.

"Okay, Lex—it's a fight you wanted, so let's get started!"

"My pleasure, Superman," Lex says as he punches the Man of Steel. Superman reels in pain.

I've always relied on my super-powers to save the day, Superman thinks as he is battered by Lex's fists. *Without them, I'm no stronger than an ordinary human! Besides, after taking that youth serum, Luthor is stronger than ever! Looks like I'm done for!* Soon Superman surrenders to Luthor's superior strength.

"I've won!" Luthor gloats. "And now I'll return to Earth—in victory! But don't worry, Superman—now that I've defeated you, my criminal days are over! Goodbye, *ex*-foe!"

Left alone for all eternity, Superman knows that Earth has lost not only its worst villain—but its greatest hero!

The End

Those doorways must lead to the next game level, Superman thinks. *I've got to make a run for one of them!*

The furry monsters chase Superman down the maze corridor, but when they see him heading for the doorway, two of the four mysteriously reverse direction. As Superman races through the doorway, only two of the monsters follow.

The tunnel is dark, except for a pinpoint of light at the exit. It grows larger as the Man of Steel approaches it.

That must be the next level! Superman thinks gratefully.

Just then, two furry forms appear at the tunnel exit. They are the two monsters that Superman thought were still in the maze!

"Oh, no!" Superman groans. "I'm trapped! I should have known that the doorways were connected!"

"Yum, yum!" the four monsters say as they grab the Man of Steel. "Eat 'em up!"

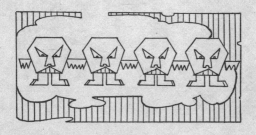

The End

"Well, I guess this is as good a way as any to get to the roof and rescue Lois," Superman says as he gets a grip on the side of the skyscraper.

After twenty minutes of climbing, the Man of Steel is exhausted, but he continues to scale the building's brick-lined surface.

About halfway up, a falling steel girder narrowly avoids hitting him. Superman gazes up toward the roof, and sees another girder heading straight for him! With only seconds to spare, Superman moves out of the way.

But then another girder is launched off the roof by Superman's unseen enemy, and then another, and another! Superman is too tired to avoid them all. He knows that both he and Lois are doomed.

The End

Superman runs down the unlit corridor until he hears someone in the darkness running toward him. In the dim light, he can hardly see who it is.

"Superman?" a strangely familiar voice says. "Is that you?" And then, from out of the shadows walks none other than—CLARK KENT!

But . . . I'm Clark Kent! Superman thinks. *This has to be another of the Toyman's robots!*

The Clark Kent robot is out of breath. "Am I glad I found you!" it puffs. "I know where Lois is!"

If Superman listens to the Clark robot, turn to page 82.

If Superman destroys the Clark robot and goes after Lois, turn to page 87.

Superman smashes through door number two and grabs Lois mere seconds before the ray can strike her.

"Superman!" Lois gasps. "How did you know which door to choose?"

"Simple," Superman answers. "The Lois robot had green eyes—but yours are definitely brown! And now I've got to stop the Toyman. With *you* out of harm's way, that will be no problem!"

Soon Superman spots the Toyman trying to make his getaway outside the factory.

"Not so fast, Toyman!" the Man of Steel shouts.

"I-I'm all out of toys to trap you!" the Toyman moans.

"Toyman," Superman grins, "the game is over."

The End

Superman pushes Lex to the ground and flees. In moments he is climbing up the side of the craggy mountain. Luthor is close behind him.

As the Man of Steel gains a foothold on one of the mountain peaks, he accidentally dislodges an enormous boulder. The huge stone begins to plummet down the side of the mountain. Superman looks down to see it heading straight toward Luthor, who is unaware of the impending doom.

If Superman warns Luthor of the danger, turn to page 115.

If Superman says nothing and allows Lex to be hit, turn to page 90.

"Sorry, Lex," Superman says, "but I won't be your delivery boy!"

"Too bad for you," Luthor says grimly, "but worse for Metropolis. The Death Ray is on its way."

Faster than the eye can follow, Superman streaks back to Metropolis, where the glowing red Death Ray is about to strike the *Daily Planet* building. With micro-seconds to spare, Superman dives in front of the deadly ray.

The beam bounces off Superman, but splinters off in a hundred different directions. Superman watches helplessly as each new beam bounces from building to building, reducing everything to ashes as it strikes. Superman knows that, within seconds, Metropolis will be nothing but smoldering rubble.

The End

Superman aims his blaster and fires. The laser beam speeds past the alien invaders and plows into the ship, causing the spacecraft to explode with a deafening roar.

The homeless aliens zip about in panic as they slowly dematerialize. Soon the lunar sky is empty once again. Then the sinister voice of the Toyman fills the icy, barren void.

"Very good, Superman. You've passed the first level. Now let's see how well you do against—this!"

Turn to page 93.

"Your friend Ms. Lane was about to expose my scheme," the Toyman says. "But with you and her out of the way, my Superman dolls will become the toy sensation of the decade!"

The mini-Supermen descend on the Man of Steel like a swarm of angry bees. Their punches sting, but do not harm the Man of Steel. Then two thousand green rays shoot out of the mini-Supermen's eyes, causing the true Superman to wince in pain. It's Green Kryptonite!

"Each of my Superman dolls has a radio-controlled, super-powered computer diode planted deep inside it," the Toyman explains as the rays continue to pelt the Man of Steel. "On Christmas morning I shall activate them all, and my dolls shall help me take over the country!"

As Superman slips into unconsciousness, he knows he will not be there to stop the Toyman's plan.

The End

Luthor hears Superman's warning and, at the last instant, ducks out of the boulder's path. But the huge rock grazes the villain's head, knocking him out. When he awakens, Luthor is tied up with alien vines found by the Man of Steel.

"Glad to see you're awake," Superman says. "We've got some loose ends to tie up, Lex. First we're going back to Earth to dismantle your Death Ray, and then *you're* going to prison!"

"All right," Luthor says, disgusted. "You won fair and square. Let's go."

In the twinkling of an eye, both are gone.

The End

At super-speed, the Man of Steel races back to the Fortress of Solitude. In the Hall of Weapons, he selects a device capable of destroying one of the Phantom Zone villains.

Select one of the following for him:

the Shrinking Ray
the box of Red Kryptonite
the Green Kryptonite Ray Gun

Superman can also decide to fight the Phantom Zone Villains without any weapon.

After selecting the weapon, Superman decides which villain he should attempt to capture.

If Superman goes after General Zod, turn to page 35.

If Superman goes after Kru-El, turn to page 36.

If Superman goes after Faora Hu-Ul, turn to page 37.

FORTRESS FILE ENTRY #1

THE TOYMAN: A criminal genius who uses toys to commit fantastic crimes. The Toyman is known to use human-sized, super-strong robots and three-dimensional holographic images to carry out his mad schemes. Warning: The Toyman is in possession of a large quantity of Green Kryptonite!

FORTRESS FILE ENTRY #2

LEX LUTHOR: Without a doubt, Lex Luthor is Superman's most dangerous foe. The bald-headed scientist became a criminal after a laboratory accident caused him to lose all his hair. Believing Superman to be responsible for his baldness, Lex Luthor will not rest until Superman is destroyed.

FORTRESS FILE ENTRY #3

FAORA HU-UL: This female Phantom Zone villainess is crazy! Her insane hatred of all mankind makes her the most dangerous of all the Phantom Zone foes. Do not approach Faora without a weapon, or you will have no chance of surviving!

FORTRESS FILE ENTRY #4

KRU-EL: This Phantom Zone villain is the strongest there is. Kru-El is not very smart, but his strength is greater than the other two Phantom Zone villains combined. Superman would be wise to use his wits to defeat Kru-El.

FORTRESS FILE ENTRY #5

GENERAL ZOD: While General Zod is hardly the strongest Phantom Zone villain, he *is* a deadly powerful enemy. Zod's main weakness is his vanity. He can never refuse a gift or a surprise. His greatest wish is to have all mankind serve his will.

ABOUT THE AUTHOR
AND ILLUSTRATOR

ANDREW HELFER was born and raised in Brooklyn, New York. He received Bachelor's degrees in English and film from the University of Rochester, and did graduate work in journalism at New York University. Mr. Helfer began his writing career during college, writing for magazines and newspapers, but has also worked as a short-order cook and a department store salesman. Currently he is a Special Projects Editor at DC Comics in New York City.

In his spare time, the author enjoys watching old cartoons and movies, playing video games, and programming computers. He also collects records, books and comic books, Japanese toy robots, and toys in general. *Superman: The Man of Steel*™ is the third book Mr. Helfer has written for young people.

JOSÉ DELBO was born and educated in Argentina, where, at the age of sixteen, he began his career as an illustrator. In 1965 he came to the United States and has lived and worked here ever since. His comic book illustrations of DC Comics Super Heroes are familiar to many people. Mr. Delbo is the artist for the daily Superman syndicated newspaper strip, and also does the artwork for the new *Superman Sunday Special* newspaper puzzle page. He lives in New Jersey with his wife and two children.